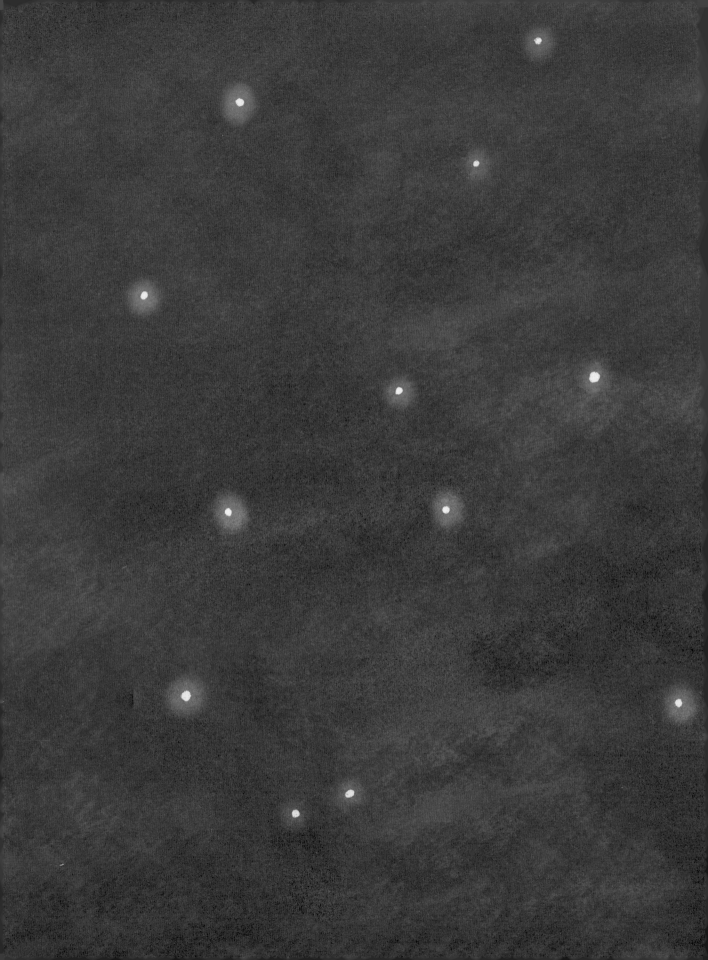

For my girls.

May you always be brave and curious.

www.mascotbooks.com

Just Like an Astronaut

For more information, please contact
Mascot Books, an imprint of Amplify Publishing Group:
620 Herndon Parkway #320
Herndon, VA 20170
info@mascotbooks.com

Library of Congress Control Number: 2022905747

CPSIA Code: PRT0422A
ISBN-13: 978-1-63755-0786

Printed in the United States

Just Like an Astronaut

Jodie Antypas (signature)

Jodie Antypas

Illustrated by Ana Sebastian

Grace had a brain that was always in overdrive. In fact, her brain hardly ever turned off. Her mind wandered to wonderfully curious places and was filled with questions that she could not ask fast enough.

How do earthquakes happen? Where does lava come from? Why is ocean water salty?

Sometimes, so much thinking led to worry, embarrassment, or shame. Grace always shared her wonders, but kept her worries to herself.

I hope nobody sees how bad my art is. I hope my science project is good enough. I bet I won't make the gymnastics team with my friends. Does anyone else feel like this?

One morning Grace announced to her mother,
"This week we are learning about outer space. I can't wait to
learn more about planets, shooting stars, and astronauts!"

As she was leaving for school, Grace demonstrated
how astronauts move through space, using her backpack
as a jetpack.

CRASH!

Dread piled up inside Grace when she saw
the vase shattered at her feet.

Before her mom could say a word, Grace darted off
to school, replaying her mistake in her head.
Mom is never going to forgive me.

Grace perked up when Mr. Raymond greeted the class. "Who's excited for outer space week? I have so many fun lessons and surprises planned!" Grace beamed as bright as an exploding supernova, forgetting about the vase.

When it was time for the lesson on planets, Grace started blurting out questions.

"Why does Jupiter have so many moons? Can humans survive on Mars? Which planets have oxygen?"

Before she could ask her next question, one of her classmates interrupted. "You are too curious! Let someone else ask a question for once!"

Grace slumped in her chair and heard snickers coming from the back of the class. Her curiosity was crushed by shame.
I ruined the lesson for everyone.

During PE, Grace and her partner were in a close game of tetherball. The ball soared so high in the air that it circled the pole just like an orbiting planet.

"Mr. Raymond, look at the tetherball orbiting…" Grace yelled just before the ball smacked her in the face.

"Are you okay?" Ruby called from the sidelines. "That must have hurt! I can't believe she didn't quit," she whispered.

But Grace kept playing and didn't answer, too mortified to admit that her face throbbed.

Grace usually walked
home from school with kids
from her neighborhood, but today
she wanted to be alone. *Mom is going
to be mad when I get home.
Everyone thinks I'm too curious.
I'm terrible in PE.*

Grace arrived home to her mom waiting with a smile. "I have an art project for you to do!" she sang.

"Glue these ceramic pieces around the edge of the frame." As she glued, Grace admired the pattern and realized that the pieces were parts of the shattered vase! *Mom still loves me, even though I made a mistake when I broke the vase!*

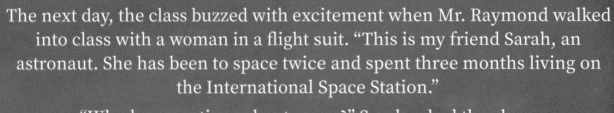

The next day, the class buzzed with excitement when Mr. Raymond walked into class with a woman in a flight suit. "This is my friend Sarah, an astronaut. She has been to space twice and spent three months living on the International Space Station."

"Who has questions about space?" Sarah asked the class.

Hands shot into the air.

"What can you eat in outer space?"

"How do you sleep without gravity?"

"How fast does the space station orbit Earth?"

Grace was bursting with questions,
but she never raised her hand.

"Can I eat lunch with you today?" the astronaut asked Grace.

"Yes!" Grace squealed. "But why do you want to eat with me?"

"I heard you are the most curious kid in the class and that you love everything about outer space, but you didn't ask any questions."

Grace's smile disappeared. "Everyone thinks I am too curious. I ruin everything with my questions."

The astronaut whispered, "All the astronauts I know are very curious. You have to ask questions if you want to learn new things!"

I am curious just like an astronaut!

During afternoon recess, Ruby called to Grace, "Come play dodgeball with us! We want you on our team."

"You want me on your team?" Grace hesitated.

"You were so brave playing tetherball yesterday that everyone wants you on their team," Ruby explained.

At the end of the day, Mr. Raymond said to the class, "Tonight's homework assignment is to write what you have learned about being an astronaut."

Homework

About the Author

Jodie is someone who has always enjoyed asking lots of questions about the world. In some cases, this natural curiosity has caused her to experience anxiety and shame, so she wrote this story to help normalize these feelings and encourage kids to recognize that something positive can result from an imperfect situation. Jodie lives in Northern California with her family.

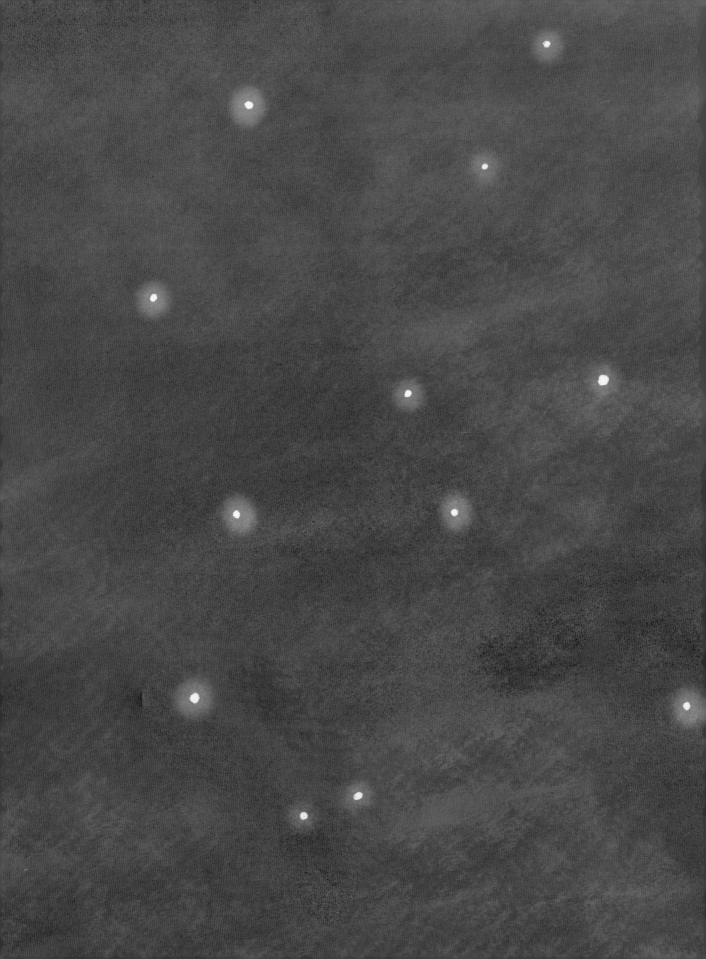